Spring's
Sparkle Sleepover

Jim Henson's Enchanted Sisters

Spring's Sparkle Sleepover

Elise Allen
and Halle Stanford

illustrated by
Paige Pooler

BLOOMSBURY
NEW YORK   LONDON   NEW DELHI   SYDNEY

This book is dedicated to Frances Hodgson Burnett.
Thank you for filling our childhoods with feisty little
heroines, fantastic frilly dresses, and the idea that a powerful
friendship is all you need to overcome adversity and bring
magic into your life. You inspired this book.

Copyright © 2015 by The Jim Henson Company, Inc.
Based on characters created by Mike Moon
Text written by Elise Allen • Illustrations by Paige Pooler
All rights reserved. No part of this book may be reproduced or transmitted in any form
or by any means, electronic or mechanical, including photocopying, recording, or by any
information storage and retrieval system, without permission in writing from the publisher.

First published in the United States of America in January 2015
by Bloomsbury Children's Books • www.bloomsbury.com

Bloomsbury is a registered trademark of Bloomsbury Publishing Plc

For information about permission to reproduce selections from this book, write to
Permissions, Bloomsbury Children's Books, 1385 Broadway, New York, NY 10018
Bloomsbury books may be purchased for business or promotional use. For information on
bulk purchases please contact Macmillan Corporate and Premium Sales Department at
specialmarkets@macmillan.com

Library of Congress Cataloging-in-Publication Data
Allen, Elise, author.
Spring's sparkle sleepover / by Elise Allen and Halle Stanford ; illustrated by Paige Pooler.
pages   cm   — (Jim Henson's Enchanted sisters)
Summary: Although Spring is nervous about her first sleepover, Winter's Snowflake Slumber
Party is great fun until a storm frightens Spring into leaving early, but she musters her
courage to lead her sisters into the Barrens when the Weeds steal Mother Nature's scepter.
ISBN 978-1-61963-269-1 (paperback) • ISBN 978-1-61963-296-7 (hardcover)
ISBN 978-1-61963-270-7 (e-book)
[1. Seasons—Fiction. 2. Nature—Fiction. 3. Magic—Fiction. 4. Stealing—Fiction.
5. Sleepovers—Fiction. 6. Sisters—Fiction.] I. Stanford, Halle, author.
II. Pooler, Paige, illustrator. III. Title.
PZ7.A42558Spr 2015   [Fic]—dc23   2014018751

Book design by John Candell • Typeset by Westchester Book Composition
Printed and bound in the U.S.A. by Thomson-Shore Inc., Dexter, Michigan
2 4 6 8 10 9 7 5 3 1 (paperback)
2 4 6 8 10 9 7 5 3 1 (hardcover)

All papers used by Bloomsbury Publishing, Inc., are natural, recyclable products
made from wood grown in well-managed forests. The manufacturing processes
conform to the environmental regulations of the country of origin.

CHAPTER
1

Braiding colorful blooms into a unicorn's mane was harder than Spring remembered. Spring wouldn't give up, though. Dewdrop, her unicorn best friend, tried to help by not moving a muscle. He lay perfectly still in Magnolia Meadow as Spring twisted a blue morning glory around a geranium that naturally grew in his silvery mane. Spring had a tradition of weaving flowery crowns on the first day of spring for those she loved most. And since the first day of spring was tomorrow, she was determined to finish this braid, no matter how difficult it was!

"Bluebells and blossoms!" she cried as her fingers tangled into yet another hopeless knot. "Dewy, I don't know why I can't do this today! It's harder than getting a ladybug to change its spots to stripes!"

Dewdrop neighed, but Spring could speak the language of all living creatures, so she heard him clear as a babbling brook. *"Have you tried getting a ladybug to change its spots to stripes?"*

"No," Spring admitted, "but sometimes I try to get my hair to change from blond waves to dark curls like Mother's. I close my eyes and concentrate as hard as I can..."

She did, then after a long moment she popped open her big violet eyes. "Did it work?"

The bouncy locks under Spring's headband were as blond as ever. *"Sorry,"* Dewdrop said.

"That's okay, I didn't think it would. Besides, I like my hair. What was I talking about again?"

"Braiding my crown," Dewdrop reminded her.

"Yes," Spring remembered. "I can't do it when my tummy's churning like gravel rolling down a hill!"

"Are you hungry?"

"No," Spring said, "it's not that. It's Winter's Snow-flake Slumber Party. It's *tonight.*"

"Why is a party churning your tummy?" Dewdrop asked. *"Aren't parties fun?"*

"Yes, but it's a *sleepover* party," Spring said.

Every year, Winter threw the Snowflake Slumber Party to celebrate the last night of winter. This year's party was special, though, because Winter, Summer, and Autumn all thought their little sister, Spring, was ready to join them and spend the night for the first time ever. Spring loved that they wanted her there, but she wasn't sure she could spend a whole night away from home.

"I've never slept anywhere but my own bed, Dewy," Spring admitted. "I'm not sure I want to go."

"*Then don't,*" Dewdrop declared. "*Stay with me instead.*"

"But if I do that, my sisters will think I'm a baby!"

"*What's wrong with being a baby?*" Dewdrop asked. "*I'm still a baby. I'm your little foal and I like to snuggle right in your lap!*"

The giant unicorn tried to curl onto her as if he were a tiny pup, and Spring squealed as she toppled over. She laughed out loud as Dewdrop's mane tickled under her chin. It made her so giggly, she had to turn away.

Spring gasped. "Dewdrop, look!"

She was nose-to-bloom with a brand-new patch of beautiful blue and white flowers. "Snowdrops!" she gushed. "They only come out when winter turns to spring! Oh, Dewdrop, they'd be perfect braided into your mane, but my fingers are as flittery as a moth's wings today." She scrunched up her mouth, thinking, and then bounced to her feet as she cried, "I have a sparkle of an idea!"

She pulled her scepter from the folds of her dress. Most of the time the glassy orb on top was a beautiful lavender, but today all but a small crescent glowed with a silvery mist. Tomorrow it would go all silver, signaling the time for the season-changing Sparkle Ceremony.

"If my fingers won't fly, I'll use a little magic and braid your mane in a Dewdrop Snowdrop Swirl!" exclaimed Spring. "Sir Dewy, please rise and lean down your head."

The beautiful violet unicorn pushed himself up by his powerful legs and bowed low as Spring had requested. The Sparkle held her scepter close and chanted:

"Snowdrops wind up in the air,
Weaving into silvery hair!
Braid, weave, entwine, and curl
Into a Dewdrop Snowdrop Swirl!"

Spring kissed the scepter's orb, then flicked it toward the ground at Dewdrop's feet. Violet sparkling light showered down on the snowdrop patch, which began to twinkle and shine. Spring had always been able to speak with all plants and creatures, but her true Sparkle Power was the ability to make living things grow. The snowdrops rose higher and higher, then wove themselves through Dewdrop's mane. When the sparkles dissolved, Dewdrop's head and neck glowed with a single, beautifully shimmering, snowdrop-swirled braid.

"Roses and robins' breasts! Dewdrop, you look positively radiant!" Spring exclaimed. "Trot over to Strawberry Creek to see your handsome reflection!"

"With pleasure," he said, and Spring laughed as Dewdrop high-kneed his way to the water. She was about to follow him when a giant sparkling rainbow

soared down from the sky and streamed right in front
of her.

Spring's sisters were coming to visit!

Summer arrived first. She slid down the rainbow
belly first, with her arms splayed like wings. Winter
surfed down right behind her, curving elaborate zig-
zags across the bands of color. Autumn floated along
last. She sat cross-legged, peacefully gliding down the
arc as she waved to Spring.

"Sparkles, I'm so happy you're here!" The minute her sisters landed, Spring hurled herself into their arms for a big group hug. "I'm so excited that tomorrow is spring! Do you want to go see all the baby animals for tomorrow's naming party?"

That was another tradition. Every first day of spring, she and her sisters went to Goldenseal Grove and named every hatchling, fawn, cub, and any other newborn creature in Spring's Sparkledom. The babies and their families were already gathering in anticipation, and Spring couldn't wait to show her sisters the cuteness.

"I'd love to see the baby animals." Autumn sighed wistfully.

"Got any jaguars?" Summer asked. Her best friend Shade was a gentle jaguar, and Summer got down on all fours to slink through the grass just like her pet.

"*Tomorrow* we can see the animals," Winter interrupted. "We're here to fetch you for the super-spectacular event *tonight*."

Spring's tummy started churning again. She'd been so excited by Dewdrop's braid and her sisters' visit, she'd forgotten all about tonight. "You mean the Snowflake Slumber Party?"

"YES!" her sisters chorused.

"And it's going to be the best Snowflake Slumber Party *ever*!" Winter exclaimed. "We'll make it the most exciting night of your life!"

"As exciting as the time I climbed the highest green vine in my Sparkledom's jungle in two minutes and twenty-six seconds flat!" Summer jumped in.

"Or as exciting as the time *I* climbed the highest pine tree in my Sparkledom's forest in two minutes and twenty-*five* seconds flat," Winter countered.

Summer's eyes gleamed. "Or as exciting as the time *I*—"

"How about it'll be as exciting as *all* of that," Autumn said, linking her arms through Summer's and Winter's, "but in a different way because it's happening for *Spring.*"

"I'll buy that," Winter said. "So what do you think, Spring? Are you as excited as a penguin belly-sledding on a giant ice slide?"

"Are you jumping out of your skin with anticipation?" Summer added.

"Are you embracing this momentous occasion signifying your leap forward toward growing Sparklehood?" asked Autumn.

Spring's tummy hurt even worse and her mouth felt dry as a desert tortoise's shell. More than ever, she knew she wasn't ready for a sleepover, but how could she tell her sisters and let them down? She forced a big smile onto her face and cried, "It'll be wintry and wondrous!"

CHAPTER
2

So let's go!" Winter crowed. "We'll start your very first Snowflake Slumber Party right now!"

"Right now?" Spring asked. "But it's so early."

"The perfect time to snowshoe up to Hullabaloo Hot Springs!" Winter said. "We'll take a dip, and then I'll reveal the first in a whole night of surprises!"

"That sounds . . . wonderful," Spring said.

It wasn't a complete lie. Spring did love Hullabaloo Hot Springs. The springs were so cozy and foamy, like vanilla soda. But how could she go to Winter's Sparkledom for the hot springs and not stay for the sleepover? Snowballs and sour grass!

"You're all packed, right, Spring?" Autumn asked.

Spring was so grateful she nearly threw her arms around Autumn. It was the perfect excuse! "No!" she cried joyfully. "I'm not packed at all!"

Realizing she sounded a little too happy about this, she cleared her throat and made her voice low and sad. "I mean, I'm not even close to packed. I can't imagine how long it will take me. Maybe you should start the sleepover without me."

"Start without you?" Summer asked. "Your very first sleepover?"

"Not a chance," Winter agreed. "Packing for a sleepover is easy. You'll take two seconds to toss everything you need in a bag, then we'll be off!"

Spring forced a smile. Winter made it sound simple, but Spring knew she could have all the time in the world and it still wouldn't be enough. Not unless she could pack her own bed . . . and her castle . . . and maybe her entire Sparkledom.

"I can't wait to slide into the hot springs," Autumn said. "I love the way the tiny bubbles tickle my skin."

"I like when the snow monkeys come to visit, and we feed them marshmallows from our mugs full of hot chocolate," Summer added.

"And then they dip their sweet potatoes in the hot springs to make them taste salty-good and get them clean!" Winter said.

"Clean!" Spring cried happily as a new idea came to her. "Sparkles, I can't go to a sleepover! I have too much spring-cleaning to do! My castle is a messy disaster!"

"It can't be that bad," Winter said. "Just leave it and clean after the party."

"But I can't!" Spring said. "Tomorrow's the first day of spring and I'll have too much to do! There's the Ceremony, and the naming party . . . It's the biggest day of the whole year in my Sparkledom, and I can't possibly enjoy it if I know my home is as cluttered as a rabbit's nest!"

"Don't you mean 'rat's nest'?" Summer asked.

"Oh, no!" Spring assured her. "All the rats I know are very tidy. It's the rabbits. They throw all their things everywhere."

"Then what they need," Winter noted, "and what *you* need, is a home that magically cleans up after itself. Like mine."

That was the last thing Spring needed. She loved puttering through all her pretty belongings and playing with them as she put them in exactly the right

spot. She had done that just yesterday and her castle was now as tidy as ... well, a rat's nest! She hated lying to her sisters, but she'd hate disappointing them even more. This was definitely the better choice.

"Maybe so," she said to Winter, "but I don't have a home like yours, so I have to clean. And it's sad because I really, really, *really* wanted to go to the sleepover. But you know how it is when you need to clean. You just gotta ... clean!"

"Spring," Autumn said with a meaningful look. "I think I know what's really going on."

Spring froze. She thought she'd been so convincing! She should have known Autumn would see right through her. "You do?" She gulped.

"Of course," Autumn said. "You need help cleaning. We're happy to chip in."

"Absolutely," Summer declared. "With all three of us it'll take no time at all."

Winter pulled out her scepter and pointed it to the sky. "Last one to Spring's castle's a melted ice cap!"

"WAIT!" screamed Spring. She needed to stall. If her sisters raced to the castle, they'd see it was perfectly clean and she'd fibbed. Sour grass and swallow-tailed kites!

Swallow-tailed . . . *kites*! Spring had an idea!

"Let's go back to my castle a different way!" she cried. "Something fun! Watch!"

Spring put two fingers in her mouth and blew a deafening whistle. A split second later, Dewdrop was at her side. His snowdrop-swirled mane still looked very fancy and he smelled like the blossoms. He and Spring nuzzled a moment, then she stepped back and pulled out her scepter.

"Leaves and flowers, weave a kite
To help my sisters soar in flight!"

Violet sparkles flew out of Spring's scepter to make a cloud around Dewdrop, the grass, and the closest trees. When the magic disappeared, Dewdrop was harnessed to a beautiful kite woven out of giant magnolia leaves and flowers.

"Snow way!" exclaimed Winter.

"A parakite!" cried Summer. "And it's big enough for all four of us!"

"All *three* of you," corrected Spring. "I'll ride on Dewdrop."

"Me too," Autumn said queasily, "if that's okay."

Dewdrop gave a delighted whinny. He had the magical ability to float on the breeze that swirled throughout Spring's Sparkledom.

"Of course!" Spring agreed. "And we'll take the long way so we can all enjoy the ride!"

And, she added to herself, *so I'll have time to figure out how to explain my perfectly tidy "mess" and still get out of going to the sleepover tonight.*

Bluebells and blossoms!

CHAPTER
3

This is AMAZING!" hooted Winter. She and Summer soared in their parakite behind Dewdrop, who galloped on top of a sparkling wind.

"Woohoooo!" cried Summer. "I'm higher than the highest mountain peak!"

"Then *I'm* higher than the highest flying animal," Winter shouted, "a bar-headed goose! Honk! Honk!"

Even Autumn was enjoying the ride. She sighed as they flew over Rosy Valley, the heart of the realm. "I always knew your Sparkledom was beautiful, Spring," she said, misty-eyed. "But from up here it's breathtaking. Thank you."

Spring wanted to be happy she made her sister so emotional, but she couldn't. The flight was only stalling the moment when her sisters saw her clean castle and realized she'd lied. Then she'd have to admit her even bigger lie and tell them she wasn't ready for the Snowflake Slumber Party.

Dewdrop banked across Glistlegloss Lake. From here Spring could see her pink Sparkle Castle, with its six orange-and-lavender towers that stretched to the sky like candles on a birthday cake. Normally the sight of it made Spring feel as safe as a tiny kitten curled up next to its mama, but now all she could think was how terrible it would be to sleep away from it tonight.

Spiders and snapdragons! If only she'd come up with a better excuse so she could stay home! One that wasn't a lie!

"Oh!" Spring blurted.

"Spring?" Autumn asked. "You okay?"

"I'm . . . I'm absolutely wonderful!" Spring cried. The perfect solution had just popped into her head! She leaned close to Dewdrop's ear and whinnied in his own language, "Dewy, take us to the Heart Garden, please."

Autumn laughed. "I love how you sound like a unicorn filly when you speak to him."

"You should hear what I sound like when I talk to snails," giggled Spring.

Dewdrop soared farther across Glistlegloss Lake, moving closer to the castle on its far shore. From up here, Spring could see all the streams that branched off its wide expanse, including one that led to Pink Dolphin Lagoon, where the Sparkles' friend Sammy the sea monster lived. Another stream flowed to the grand river that twisted through each of the sisters' Sparkledoms.

As Dewdrop glided down toward the castle, every creature and plant raised its voice in welcome.

"*Hello!*" chorused a patch of wildflowers.

"*Welcome home, Spring!*" chittered a cluster of butterflies.

"*Hooray for Spring and her Sparkle Sisters!*" rustled the clover grass.

"Thank you, thank you!" Spring said, blowing kisses to all of them. "Autumn, everything is saying hello!"

"Really?" Autumn asked, then waved and shouted, "Hello, everything!"

Dewdrop touched down in the middle of a garden, in a heart-shaped courtyard, in the center of the castle. This was Spring's Heart Garden and everywhere dozens of blue, yellow, and pink rosebushes were sculpted into perfect heart shapes. Each individual rose also grew naturally in the shape of a perfect valentine heart.

"What a ride!" Summer cried as she and Winter shrugged off their magnolia kite.

"Not too bumpy for you?" Winter chided her.

"Not even a little!" Summer retorted. "Why, was it too bumpy for *you*?"

" 'Course not," Winter said. She playfully nudged Summer with her elbow.

"It was a little bumpy for *me*," Autumn admitted, "but it was a lot of fun."

Spring would have loved to chat along with her sisters, but she had a mission to accomplish. She pointed her scepter at a rosebush filled with sumptuous orange blossoms and chanted:

"Roses take me to my room,
Grow as fast as you can zoom!"

Violet sparkles showered the rosebush, which began growing at an incredible speed. The roses wove into a chair of soft blooms and lifted her high into the air.

"Spring!" Autumn cried. "Where are you going?"

"I want to get a jump on my room before you see it!" Spring called down. "I could use a little time, so please grab a snack in the kitchen! It's lemon sugar cookie day!"

All the Sparkles had kitchens that magically provided the girls' favorite foods. Her kitchen's lemon sugar cookies were particularly delicious, and she hoped they'd distract the Sparkles for a while.

Spring hadn't lied to them. She *was* going to get a jump on her room, but she wasn't going to clean it. She was going to mess it up.

The flowery chair grew all the way up to the high balcony outside her bedroom, then deposited her on her feet. "Thank you, sweet roses," Spring said.

"*Our pleasure, Spring,*" they answered.

Spring raced into her bedroom, which she loved more than anyplace in the world. Its soft green carpet smelled like freshly cut grass. Live cherry trees grew out of the lavender-colored walls, their branches bursting with ever-blooming pink blossoms. Parasols painted with spring flowers dangled from the ceiling, as did a low swing that hung from leafy vines.

In the middle of it all sat her snuggly bed, with the headboard shaped exactly like her pink castle.

The only problem with the room was that it was clean, and she needed it to be messy so that she could back up her "messy room story" to her sisters. That, and get out of the Snowflake Slumber Party. She leaped onto her lilac lounging chair, pointed her scepter here and there, and quickly whispered:

"Let this room be neat no more,
Tangle, unmake, and throw on the floor!"

A cyclone of violet sparkles blew through Spring's room. They swept over her pink-glass-topped crafting table, popping open drawers and exploding scraps of lace, feathers, and colored pencils everywhere. Spring's blankets, sheets, and pillows jumped up when the sparkles hit them, then wrestled with one another until the bedclothes were in a knot and the pillows had burst their stuffing.

Spring giggled. Already her room was shaping up into a fine catastrophe!

But the magic wasn't finished. Next, the sparkling twister blasted open the doors to Spring's boudoir— a fancy Outworld name for a dressing room—and rocketed Spring's taffeta dresses, silk slippers, and velvet ribbons through the air like a startled flock of birds. Spring squealed as a giant yellow bonnet smacked into her, knocked her off balance, and toppled her into a pile of gowns, gloves, and other clothing just as Summer knocked on the door.

"Spring, it's us!" she called. "We're here to help you clean!"

As Spring crawled out from the pile of clothes, she heard her sisters open the door and come in.

"Wow, Spring," Winter groaned. "This place is a disaster!"

Spring blushed. She knew she'd messed up the room on purpose, but Winter didn't. She felt Winter wasn't being very nice. "You don't have to be mean about it," she said.

Winter, Autumn, and Summer had been staring at the chaos, but now they turned to Spring ... and burst out laughing! Spring's face burned. "Now none of you are being nice!"

"It's not that," Autumn assured her. "I'm sorry. It's just . . . you have . . . *things* on you."

Spring glanced in the mirror. Somehow she'd emerged from the pile of clothes with several flowery undergarments static-stuck to her dress. And to her hair. Spring's cheeks blushed even redder. She shook off the underwear and straightened her skirt.

"You and this room." Winter chuckled. "Are you sure you're not going Weed on us?"

This was too much. The Weeds were the Sparkles' worst enemies. They were troublemaking boys who lived with their leader, Bluster Tempest, in the Barrens, the wild and chaotic land surrounding the Sparkledoms. They were always scheming to try and steal the sisters' magical scepters and headbands. They also lived like filthy, disgusting slobs. How could Winter possibly compare her to them?

Spring was about to tell her sisters how sparkling her room had been just moments ago, but then Summer added, "With your room like this, no wonder you haven't packed for the sleepover yet."

The sleepover. That's why Spring had to be patient and let her sisters criticize her. This was her way out of the sleepover. She bit her lip and shrugged apologetically. "I guess I let things get a little out of control. Sorry it's messing up our plans."

"It won't mess up our plans at all," Autumn said.

"It won't?" Spring asked.

"Absolutely not. The room is messy, but it's nothing a little sisterly Sparkle Power can't fix." Autumn raised her scepter and called:

"Autumn winds be my broom,
Swiftly clean this unkempt room!"

Red and orange sparkles swirled into the air, and warm breezes blew in from all directions. *SWISH! SWASH! SWOOSH!* Spring's garments and accessories flitted into the air, folded themselves neatly, and gently soared back to their proper spots. Her bedclothes detangled themselves and spread themselves neatly back into place. Even the dust whooshed out the window, leaving the floor spotless.

"Done!" Autumn said. "And good as new."

"So now we can get you packed!" Summer added.

"And finally start your very first sleepover!" Winter crowed.

"How ... wonderful!" Spring tried to sound enthusiastic, but inside she was devastated. She wished she could just tell her sisters she wanted to stay home, but she liked that they *thought* she was ready for a slumber party, even if she really wasn't. She reluctantly pulled out her favorite tote bag—the one topped with hot-pink finch feathers—and numbly placed items inside as a million questions tumbled through her head. *What would it be like to sleep in another bedroom? Wouldn't she miss her fluffy purple comforter? What if it was too dark in Winter's Sparkledom? What if she couldn't see the moon, her natural night-light?*

"Spring, why are you packing your rain boots?" asked Autumn.

Spring was surprised to see them in her hands. She really had been distracted. "Um . . . in case I dream about rain?"

"Makes sense to me," Winter said with a shrug. Summer nodded as well.

"Then all you need now is something to sleep with that makes you feel safe and cozy," Autumn said. "I packed my stuffed elephant, which looks exactly like Whisper. I call her Beatrice."

"I always pack my first beach blanket, from when I was little," said Summer.

"And I have special fuzzy socks I bring to every sleepover," Winter added. "But, since tonight's sleepover is at my house, I may not need them."

Spring looked around the room. Could she pack *everything* in her tote bag? Maybe just her Daisy Dolly. But if she brought Daisy Dolly, wouldn't Rose Petal Bear be lonely?

Then she saw it—her favorite pillow. It was embroidered with unicorns, so it would remind her of her room *and* of Dewdrop. This might be exactly what she needed to fall asleep in a new place. "I have it!" she cried, hugging her pillow to her heart. "My pillow will be safe and cozy!"

"It's perfect," Autumn agreed.

"Good!" Winter exclaimed. "Then we can finally go!"

She led the way out to the balcony. Spring held her pillow and grabbed the tote bag and the small purple pouch of seeds she always wore around her neck when she left her Sparkledom. It was a habit she'd started after she and her sisters had gotten trapped in the Barrens. Spring had wanted to use her Sparkle Power, but with no living plants around, she couldn't make things grow. With the pouch around her neck, she always had a smattering of seeds to grow into all kinds of useful items.

Spring joined her sisters on the balcony and took a deep breath.

I can do this, she told herself. *I can ride the rainbow to Winter's and start the sleepover. I'm ready. I even have my unicorn pillow!*

She and her sisters pulled out their scepters and called in unison:

"Rainbow, rainbow, reunite,
Fly on colored wings of light!
Now that all the cleaning's done,
Snowflake Slumber Party, here we come!"

Like synchronized ballerinas, each Sparkle gracefully touched her scepter orb to her headband gem. Rainbow light soared from the gems and joined together to make a colorful pathway to the sky.

"Hooray for Spring's first sleepover!" called Summer as she cartwheeled up the rainbow.

"And a last night of winter to remember!" added Winter, somersaulting into the sky.

"After you, Spring," Autumn offered. "It's your special night."

Spring wanted to obey. She wanted to dive up the rainbow as eagerly as her sisters. She wanted to giggle and drink hot chocolate in Hullabaloo Hot Springs. She wanted to enjoy all Winter's surprises. She wanted her sisters to see her as grown-up as they were.

But she didn't want to say good-bye to her room.

"Spring?" asked Autumn.

"I just remembered one last thing I need to do," Spring said. "I'll be quick as a hummingbird and meet you there."

"Are you sure?" Autumn asked. "I'm happy to wait."

"Positive," Spring said. "You can tell Winter and Summer I'll be right over."

"If you're sure. See you soon!" Autumn majestically raised her arms and soared into the rainbow.

Spring felt small as she watched her sisters disappear into the distance. *Now I know what the last baby bird to leave the nest feels like.* She hiccuped a little sob . . . then stepped away from the rainbow's glow. She would ride it soon, but not to Winter's Sparkledom. Before she could even think about sleeping away from home, she needed extra help.

She needed her mother.

CHAPTER
4

Spring counted to ten by water lilies after her sisters left (one water lily, two water lily, three water lily . . .), then conjured the rainbow again and asked it to take her directly to Mother Nature. As she soared down to Mother's Sparkledom, the perfect blend of all the seasons, every plant and animal greeted her in its own language. Spring answered each and every one of them.

She touched down in the tropical Choral Cloud Forest. Next to her was a strangler fig tree whose ropy trunk Mother Nature had coaxed into the shape of an enormous, spiraling aviary. Spring raced inside, and marveled at all the different creatures. Pink fluorescent cockatoos mingled with acorn woodpeckers, and flocks of sparrows danced with jewel-colored hummingbirds.

What she didn't see was Mother Nature. Had the rainbow delivered her to the wrong part of the Sparkledom?

"Mother! Where are you?" cried Spring. "I need you!"

"So I understand," said a comforting voice. "But what could possibly have my dear Spring in such a tangle the night before her favorite day of the year?"

The voice sounded like Mother's, but when Spring turned to face it, all she saw was a large rainbow-plumed bird.

"Mother?" Spring asked.

The bird turned. It *was* Mother. She wore a beautiful gown with a long skirt and train of green-and-blue peacock plumes, and a bodice of small blue and pink feathers. Long yellow feathers draped from her arms like wings, and perched amid her black curls, eye-poppingly green quetzal feathers framed her ever-present headpiece and gem. "You called, my dear?"

Spring ran into her arms and breathed in her scent of salty oceans and cedarwood. "Mother, I thought you were a rare bird!"

"It's not the first time I've been called that," Mother admitted with a wink. "Now tell me. What's muddling you up this lovely last day of winter?"

"It's Winter's Snowflake Slumber Party," Spring said, twiddling her skirt. "My sisters decided I'm old enough to go this year...

but I don't know if I want to. I mean, I *want* to, but..."

"But you're not sure you're ready?"

Relief flooded through Spring. Mother always knew exactly how she felt. She nodded.

"Did you tell your sisters?" Mother asked.

"I couldn't," Spring admitted. "We've been planning this so long, they'd be disappointed. And..."

She looked up at Mother, whose eyes were so filled with love and understanding that Spring knew she could reveal even her deepest fears.

". . . and I was afraid they'd think I was a baby."

"That was very brave of you to admit," Mother said. "I can tell it weighed on you."

Mother was right. Spring hadn't even realized how hard it had been to keep everything in until she'd confessed her true feelings. She suddenly felt as light as a bit of dandelion fluff.

"Hello, Mother! And welcome, Spring!" cooed a giant blue dove as she swooped into the aviary. It was Serenity, Mother's most trusted advisor. She spoke in her own bird language, which Mother could understand as well as Spring. *"I've come to check on Game Night preparations. Shall I see to the food and drink?"*

"That would be very helpful, Serenity," said Mother Nature. "Black sesame cakes and silver green tea, if you will. And please make sure the tea is *extra* bitter. You know how my guest likes it."

"Will do! Cooo-COOOOOO!" Serenity called as she flew out the aviary skylight, instantly blending into the blue sky.

"Now back to you and your dilemma," Mother

said. "I find it's often easier to think when you're doing. Will you help me finish feeding the birds?"

"I'd love to," Spring said.

"Good." Mother Nature pointed her scepter at Spring, and a smattering of barley seeds appeared on Spring's shoulders. Almost instantly, a dozen finches swooped down and perched on her to enjoy the feast. The feel of their tiny feet and lightly pecking beaks made Spring giggle.

"Your laughter is a sound I love," said Mother Nature. "Now tell me, what is it about the sleepover that concerns you?"

"Well, I've never slept anywhere else but my bed. And I'm afraid I won't fall asleep. That's why I brought my pillow from home." Slipping the tote bag off her shoulder, she pulled out her special unicorn pillow.

"That was clever thinking," remarked Mother Nature.

"Autumn suggested it. But I'm not sure it'll be enough to help."

"Is there anything else that would help you a little

more?" Mother asked as she held out a handful of seeds to several hungry flamingos.

Spring closed her eyes and concentrated hard until the answer hit her. "A night-light! In my Sparkledom there's a beautiful full moon every night. I can see it from my bed, and it always makes me feel happy and safe before I fall asleep."

"Moongazing before bed makes me feel happy and safe too," Mother Nature said.

"Really?" Spring gaped. She couldn't imagine Mother ever feeling anything *but* happy and safe.

"Of course," Mother said. "The moon is very comforting. In fact . . . what if you could bring the moon with you to Winter's Snowflake Slumber Party?"

"Woodchips and whip-poor-wills!" Spring cried. "I can't fit the moon into my tote bag!"

"Can't you?" Mother asked mysteriously. "Come with me, Spring. I have something I want to give you. We need to hurry, though. My Game Night with Bluster Tempest is starting soon, and I hate to keep him waiting. It makes him very angry, and he enjoys that far too much."

Mother quickly strode out of the aviary along a suspension bridge made of vines, and Spring hurried after her. "Your Game Night is with *Bluster Tempest*?" Spring squeaked.

Bluster Tempest was, without a doubt, the scariest person Spring had ever known. With his terrible magic, the man could conjure up the fiercest sandstorm or crack open mountains with a mighty earthquake. Had Mother really invited him to her Sparkledom?

"Oh, Bluster's all bluster," Mother said, "and I do love to watch him go into hysterics when he loses. After all, as I've told you, I consider him a dear friend."

Mother *had* told Spring and the Sparkles that before, but it was so hard to believe. Spring wanted to ask Mother more about it, but their path was suddenly blocked by a thick wall of mist. Mother waved her arm and the mists parted to reveal a gigantic cave opening. It looked like a cracked geode with glowing crystals inside.

"Sparkles and surprises!" gasped Spring. "Is this . . . your Jeweled Cave?"

"Indeed it is, Spring. You are as clever as a spider spinning a web. Would you like to come inside?"

Spring was speechless. She and her sisters had heard about this magical place where Mother kept her most precious treasures, but none of them had ever seen it. Spring tried to look in every direction at once as she followed Mother into the cave. Giant yellow, pink, and white crystals jutted out from every wall in a wild spiked kaleidoscope. Spring felt tiny as an ant as she and Mother turned down a hallway where indigo crystals grew large and smooth like oversized birch leaves, passed a cavern of frozen crystal waterfalls, skirted glowing pools swimming with diamond koi fish, and finally emerged into an underground gem garden.

Mother Nature glided to a patch of shimmering amethyst flowers. Cuddled around the blossoms were tiny boxes and large chests made of glass, shells, geodes, porcelain, and precious woods. Mother picked up a blue lapis box inlaid with a silver sun, moon, and stars. She handed it to Spring.

"Open it," Mother suggested.

Trembling with excitement, Spring lifted the lid. Inside nestled a silver necklace threaded through with a moonstone pendant as big as a cherry. The stone glowed with radiant blue fire.

"Moonstones and magic!" shouted Spring gleefully. "Is this really for me?"

"It is," explained Mother Nature. She clasped the bauble around Spring's neck, being careful not to tangle it with the seed pouch already hanging there. "Whenever you need a little light this evening, just

hold the moonstone in the palm of your hand and whisper: *Little moon, shine bright. Give me comfort in the night.*"

Spring held the moonstone in her palm. It felt cool to the touch.

"Go ahead," Mother urged. "Try it."

Spring whispered the magic phrase. As she finished, the moonstone glowed in a luminous sphere that burst out of the necklace and hovered over her hand. Spring was delighted!

"When you want the light to return to the moonstone," instructed Mother Nature, "cup the little moon in your hands and whisper: *Good night, sweet light.*"

Spring did, and with a flash of blue sparkle, the necklace returned to normal.

"Thank you, Mother!" cried a jubilant Spring as she hugged her mom tight. "With a magical nightlight like this, I *know* I can sleep at Winter's Snowflake Slumber Party! You are the best mother in all the Sparkledoms, the Outworld, and Outer Space!"

GURGLE!

A loud rumbling filled the underground cavern, and Spring laughed a tinkle-bell giggle when she realized it was her own tummy. She'd been so worried about the Snowflake Slumber Party, she hadn't eaten since last night.

Mother laughed too. "That is the sound of a very hungry Sparkle, and I certainly can't send you to your first sleepover on an empty stomach. Come join Bluster and me for a snack."

A snack with Mother sounded wonderful, but with Bluster Tempest? "Do I have to?"

"Oh, Spring," Mother cooed. "You don't have to be afraid of Bluster. Remember what I taught you about him and his Weeds?"

"They help keep the Outworld in balance, just like us," Spring answered reluctantly. "Thunderbolts, twisters, and quakes are as much a part of nature as flowers and waterfalls."

"Exactly," Mother said. "Bluster can be naughty at times, but he's actually quite amusing once you get to know him. He is also quite good at cyclone checkers. Just not as good as me."

"Do you *blow* him away?" Spring asked playfully.

"Indeed I do," said Mother Nature. "But it's Bluster's own fault. He's too impatient. If you take your time to plan your moves, he gets so frustrated that he reacts too quickly and makes mistakes. Then he grows as irritated as a hornet trapped under glass."

Spring laughed out loud imagining a tiny Bluster buzzing around inside a glass. Suddenly a snack with him was much less scary.

"Remember this, Spring," Mother said. "Laughing is another good way to face your fears."

Spring giggled. "Then between Bluster and the sleepover, I'm going to need to tell a whole lot of jokes today!"

CHAPTER
5

After they left the caves, Spring walked hand in hand with Mother along the seashore until they stood facing a sandy island in the shape of a sea turtle. Resting on the turtle's back was an enchanting white stone villa topped with sky-blue domes and golden weather vanes. This was Mother Nature's home.

As Mother stepped out into the water, a pathway of shells rose to the surface to guide her and Spring's way to the villa, which was filled with tiled stairways that led to multiple levels, numerous balconies, and verandas to the east and west. Normally Spring would skip her way to Mother's sitting room, but her feet disliked Bluster as much as the rest of her. She stuck close by Mother Nature, half-hidden by Mother's skirts.

"Good day, everyone!" Mother declared as she entered the room. "I see my guest of honor hasn't arrived."

At that happy news, Spring leaped out to romp around the room and gaze at everything. There was always something new and exciting in Mother's sitting room. Today, six meerkats sat at an antique card table playing a lively game of Go Fish. Near them, a group of geese cornered a fox in a game of Fox & Geese on a life-size checkerboard. At the other end of the room, a pack of Pekingese pups challenged several ferns in bowling, while four small, spiny brown hedgehogs rolled themselves as shooters in a game of marbles. Overseeing it all sat Serenity, perched on one of the hanging globes that mapped out the Spar-kledoms and the Outworld.

GURGLE!

Spring's tummy roared so loudly, she thought every animal would stop and stare.

"My!" Mother exclaimed. "That belly cannot wait another second to be filled." She waved her scep-ter at a spot on the dark wood-paneled floor. A smattering of blue sparkles glittered down and grew into a bush that flowered with Spring's favorite snacks: petite carrot muffins, mini pea pies, and giant golden raspberries. The Sparkle ate as fast as her little fingers could pluck. Everything tasted so fresh that she wished she could savor every bite, but she desperately wanted to finish and run before Bluster Tempest arrived.

Yet just as she popped a final raspberry into her mouth, a massive black tornado swirled toward Mother's villa. The wind rattled the clocks and musical instruments on the wall. Everyone turned to stare except Spring, who quickly scampered under a billiard table. She closed her eyes, but there was no escaping the terrible racket as the storm bullied its way into the sitting room. She heard playing cards whisked off tables, hanging globes banging into one another, books slamming off their shelves, and vases smashing onto the floor. One crashed so close to her hiding spot that Spring had to open her eyes and scurry away from the broken glass. When she did, she saw a black funnel cloud unwind itself to reveal the man at its core: Bluster Tempest.

"Salivations and salutations!" shouted Bluster, his

arms flung up like the wings of a landing vulture. He paced the room as he twisted his waxed black mustache with spindly fingers. To Spring, his dark cape, top hat, and hair made him look like a patch of black fungus.

"Mistress Mother Nature, may a thousand antelopes fertilize your humble home," said Bluster in a voice that dripped like greasy corn oil. "You are even more bountiful and beautiful than last I laid my stunning eyes upon you."

"Bluster, I just saw you yesterday for our weekly walk," said Mother Nature.

"Was it only yesterday? Ah, handsome me. What is time to a gentleman like myself, who would delight in seeing every timepiece in the world smashed to smithereens?"

"Always the charmer, Bluster," said Mother Nature. "Please, allow me to take your cape. Now that you're here, Game Night can officially begin. After one little task, of course."

Mother Nature waved her hands and every toppled, tumbled, and shattered item repaired itself and

returned to its proper place. Then Bluster's cape rose off of his shoulders and onto a tree-shaped coatrack by the door.

"I preferred it the other way," Bluster mused, "but I suppose this will do." He reached into his double-breasted vest and pulled out a large heart-shaped box. "A hostess gift." He offered it to Mother Nature. "May it entice your taste buds like the nectar of a Venus flytrap does a small, unsuspecting insect."

"Bluster, how thoughtful!" Mother Nature opened the box to reveal several cream-filled chocolates. "My favorite. You always remember."

"Manners matter," said Bluster Tempest through smiling teeth.

"That's what I always say," Mother noted. "And I'd be quite unmannerly if I didn't offer one of these to my daughter. Spring, would you like a chocolate?"

Mother bent over to offer the box, as if there were nothing unusual about a Sparkle crouching beneath the billiard table during Game Night.

"Spring?" Bluster lilted. "Under the table?"

He popped his head down to take a peek. His black eyes lit up like a lightning storm and he curled his mustache above his toothy grin. Spring tried not to scream.

"Indeed it is!" exclaimed Bluster. "The youngest Sparkle in the flesh! Why, you look as darling as a little worm cowering in a pile of dirt. Surely you're not down there hiding from me."

Frightened as Spring was, she didn't like Bluster's tone. It sounded like he was making fun of her, and she did *not* want to give him the satisfaction of being correct. She climbed out from under the table and stood with her hands on her hips. She remembered what Mother had said about laughter helping when you were scared.

"What do you call it when worms take over the Outworld?" she blurted.

Bluster looked as confused as a wolf who received a salad for lunch.

"I don't know," he said. "What *do* you call it when worms take over the Outworld?"

"Global worming!" exclaimed Spring.

Bluster Tempest stared wide-eyed at Spring for an icy moment and then burst out laughing. "Two of my favorite things in one joke!" he guffawed. "Worms and global warming. Well done, Spring. I must say, I always found your season to be so sickly sweet with its baby birds and daffodils. But there is more to you than meets the eye."

"Much more," Mother agreed.

Spring felt a warm rush of pride. Two adults were saying they were impressed by her. Maybe she *was* growing up.

"One more thing," Spring told Bluster bravely. "You said I looked like a worm cowering in a pile of dirt, but that's not possible. Worms don't *cower* in dirt. It's their home and where they go to stay warm."

"I stand corrected," Bluster said. "Tell me, Spring, would you like to stay and join your mother and me for a game of cyclone checkers? Be warned—I do cheat."

"I'm afraid Spring has other things on her agenda today," Mother jumped in. "She's going to a Snowflake Slumber Party."

"How chilling!" Bluster enthused. "Do have a good time. And if you ever do wish to join a Game Night, I believe I would be most entertained by your company."

Spring wasn't sure whether that was a compliment or not, but she thanked him just in case. As she gave Mother a hug and turned to leave, Bluster cleared his throat.

"Speaking of worms, Spring, tell me—how can you tell which end of a worm is which?"

"How?" she asked.

"Tickle it in the middle and see which end laughs!" said Bluster Tempest. He let out a series of loud guffaws. He sounded like a crazy donkey, and soon Spring was giggling too. She couldn't believe it. All she did was stand up to him, and now they were laughing together and he'd invited her to play games! If she could handle Bluster this well, a simple Snowflake Slumber Party with the sisters she adored would be nothing!

As Spring skipped out to the sunset-lit terrace and summoned the rainbow, she heard one last bellow from Bluster.

"Serenity," he summoned, "do be a turtledove and bring me a cup of tea. *Extra bitter.*"

CHAPTER
6

Brownie Pops!"

The four Sparkle Sisters were in Winter's kitchen, still chilled from their dash back from Hullabaloo Hot Springs. They sat in a cozy booth and marveled over the treats laid out on the table: brownie Pops, colorful bowls of frosting, snowflake-shaped sprinkles, crumbled peppermints, and roasted nuts for dipping.

"I'm going to coat mine in pink frosting and *all* the toppings!" Spring cried.

"Me too!" Summer agreed.

"I'm going to keep mine simple, just as it is," said Autumn.

"Nothing simple!" Winter shot back. "Not at a Snowflake Slumber Party. You have to try at least three different toppings."

"Maybe two," Autumn relented. She smeared vanilla frosting on her Brownie Pop and coated it with the littlest bit of peppermint.

"So tell me, Spring, on a scale of cold to hot, cold of course being the best, how would you rate your first sleepover?" asked Winter.

"Icy cold!" said Spring. She smiled a huge grin, and all her sisters hooted and guffawed. "What?" she asked.

"You have something in your teeth!" Summer laughed. Her smile was also coated in chocolate and frosting.

"So do you!" Spring tittered.

"What about me?" asked Winter. She smiled wide to show the chocolate brownie she'd purposely smeared all over her teeth. "Do my teeth look like the Weeds'?"

"YES!" Summer and Spring said with a laugh.

"No," countered Autumn. "They look worse. They look like Bluster's!"

All the sisters howled with laughter until their breath hiccuped out in gasps.

"Okay," Winter said when she could speak again.

"Spring, you said this sleepover so far is icy cold—which is pretty cool—but I bet my next plan will make it fabulously frigid! We'll get ready for bed and have a pajama dance party!"

"I'd love that!" Spring cried. She'd always heard about her sisters' pajama dance parties and couldn't wait to have one herself.

"Let's go up to my bedroom and change," Winter said. "I call the hard way!"

She skated across her icy floor to the sledding hill that rolled down from the second story. As she started to scramble up, Summer raced after her, crying, "I call the hard way too!"

"*I* call the easy way," Autumn told Spring. "Want to join me?"

Spring very much did, and followed Autumn to the long pole that ran the entire height of the chalet, from the bottom floor all the way up to Winter's bedroom. Winter liked to jump on it and slide down, but how could they ride it up?

"Are you sure this is the easy way?" Spring asked.

"Hold tight to my waist," instructed Autumn. She pulled out her scepter and commanded:

"Winter winds I do cajole
To lift us swiftly up this pole!"

A breeze swirling with Sparkle magic lifted the girls off of their feet and rocketed them up the pole. *Whip-poor-wills and waterspouts!* Spring thought. *Now I know what a geyser feels like!*

Once they reached Winter's bedroom, Autumn jumped back from the pole, and she and Spring landed in a pile of giant, fluffy white pillows. Spring barely had a second to catch her breath when one of the pillows licked her! Startled, she squealed and sputtered, then realized she was nose-to-nose with the world's largest polar bear.

"Flurry!" she exclaimed. She threw her arms around Winter's pet polar bear and kissed his wet black nose, but Flurry wanted to play. He toppled Spring over and licked her face with his sloppy blue tongue.

"Ew-ew-ew!" giggled Spring.

She rolled away from Flurry's tongue bath and instead found the snowflake-shaped spot on his belly where he loved to be scratched.

"Hey, Flurrball!" shouted Winter as she and Summer raced into the room. "Get over here and let's wrestle!"

Flurry roared and bounded to Winter. On the way, he dented one of the stilts holding up Winter's sky-bed, knocked over a fuzzy couch, and toppled a Hula-Hoop rack. The room shimmered with Sparkle magic as everything fixed and righted itself. Spring couldn't even imagine what Winter's chalet would look like without its magic power to put itself back together.

As Spring watched Flurry and Winter gleefully roughhouse, she couldn't help but think about Dewdrop. She missed her unicorn. He didn't roughhouse, he cuddled. He was probably nestled in his warm bed of hay, listening to the sounds of the crickets by the river. Spring wondered if he missed her too.

"Oh, Winter, are these tents for us?" Autumn sounded entranced, and when Spring followed her gaze, she saw four white tents in the shape of igloos, each one glowing from the inside. They looked like magical paper lanterns, fragile and beautiful.

Winter peeked out from under Flurry's fuzzy

arms. "Better believe it," she said. "One silky sleepover tent for each of us! What do you think, Spring?"

"Winter, they're ... *enchanting*," Spring cooed. "Can we go inside?"

"Yes!" Winter enthused. "I want to know if you love it!"

Spring crawled over the pink butterfly welcome mat in front of her igloo. The gossamer interior was lit up with glass snow-balls glowing with an array of colors, like the northern lights that she knew their season-changing Ceremony created for the Outworlders. Her finch-feather tote bag sat right next to a downy pile of white fuzzy blankets, and her unicorn pillow lay on top, exactly where it belonged. Spring lay down on it and again thought about Dewdrop. He would love this wondrous tent. She wished he was with her and they could spend the night in it together.

"Let's all get dressed in our pajamas for the dance party!" Summer's voice rang out.

"Okay!" Spring called.

Getting ready for the dance party took Spring's mind off bedtime, and how sad it would be to sleep so far from Dewdrop and home. She pulled on her satiny nightgown with the purple butterflies, tucked her seed pouch and moonstone necklace under the collar, and put on her candy-pink slippers.

"Is everyone dressed?" called Winter.

A chorus of yeses rang out, then Winter shouted, "Hit it, Flurry!"

The bear tapped a drumroll on the floor with his paws, and followed that with a percussive dance rhythm drummed on the floor and walls. He tapped his claws on the light fixture to make the sound of a cymbal.

"Now!" Winter called, and all four Sparkles burst out of their igloos, striking dramatic poses to show off their outfits. Summer wore her favorite green tiger-striped pajamas. Autumn's red robe flapped dramatically around a long yellow nightgown laced with fan-shaped gingko tree leaves. Her bare feet were adorned with golden toe rings, and her unbraided hair flowed down her back in an ebony waterfall. Winter wore white cashmere long johns, a hoodie with pom-pom ties, and teal-blue boots. Jingle bells jangled whenever she moved.

Flurry kicked up the tempo of his drumming and all the Sparkles danced around the room. Autumn swayed slowly and sinuously, Summer turned somersaults and headstands, Winter flailed with wild abandon, and Spring twirled in dizzying circles. They danced until they were completely out of breath, then dissolved into an exhausted pile of giggles. Spring was elated. If this was what a sleepover was all about, she couldn't wait for the next one!

"And now," Winter said when she caught her breath, "for

the next event of the evening: we'll put our hair in rag curls. Then by morning we'll all have hairdos like Spring's."

"Like mine?" Spring echoed. She touched her hair, flattered and amazed that her sisters would want to imitate her simple loose curls.

"Of course," Autumn said. "It's a perfect way to ring in your season."

"And then," Winter said, "it'll be time for my biggest surprise of the night. We'll go outside, tell super-spooky stories, and curl up to sleep inside my insanely ice-tacular snow fort!"

Summer's and Autumn's eyes grew wide with excitement, but all Spring's happiness squeezed out of her like she was a juiced lemon. She'd been doing so well, but the thought of telling spooky stories outside . . . of *sleeping* outside . . .

Cobwebs and cockleshells! What was she going to do?!

CHAPTER
7

"Is everyone ready for spoooooky stories?" Winter asked. She leaned close to the crackling fire so the light danced eerily over her face. All four Sparkles had their hair in rag curlers. Spring had hoped that doing their hair would be so fun her sisters might forget about going out to the snow fort, but now here they were, huddled around a campfire as eerie shadows climbed the icy walls.

Spring didn't like spooky stories anywhere. Out here, she wanted no part of them at all.

"Maybe we should play a game first," she suggested.

"But that wasn't part of my plan." Winter sounded disappointed.

"That's okay," Summer said. "Adding in a game will just stretch the sleepover longer!"

"Exactly," Autumn agreed. "We can play Truth or Tickle—you tell the absolute truth, or you get tickled."

"Fine," Winter said, "then I'll start. Truth or tickle to Autumn. What is the naughtiest thing you have ever done?"

Autumn stared into the fire, her lips pursed together. It took her so long to answer that Spring could only imagine how very naughty her answer must be.

"Once," whispered Autumn, "I ate an entire bunch of grapes before they were ready to be harvested."

"That's a lie!" Winter crowed. "Everyone tickle her!"

Winter lunged for Autumn, but Autumn ducked out of her way.

"It's true!" Autumn protested. "I mean, I did blow away Mother's blanket for Serenity, but that was an accident. The grapes I ate on purpose."

"Look at her face, Winter," Summer said. "I think she's telling the truth."

"I *am*," Autumn insisted, "which means it's my turn. Summer, truth or tickle: if you had to kiss one of the Weeds . . . which one would it be?"

"Ewwww!" Winter erupted.

"Ugh!" Summer roared.

"Autumn, how could you even *ask* that?" squealed Spring.

"It's the game!" Autumn answered. "The questions are supposed to be hard. Summer?"

"The truth?" Summer said. "I'd rather kiss a slug than a Weed."

"Me too," Spring said. "I have some very good slug friends."

"I believe you," Winter told Summer, "but that doesn't answer the question. So unless you want to be tickled..."

"Fine!" exclaimed Summer. "If I *had* to choose... not Sleet. He's too cold, inside and out. Twister has terrible breath, even worse than the others. Quake... ugh, he's dirty, all the time. So I guess... I guess I'd choose Thunderbolt."

"*Thunderbolt?*" her sisters all roared.

"I didn't say I *want* to kiss him!" countered Summer. "Autumn said if I *had* to! I agree, he's awful, but he's better than the rest of them."

"I bet you just want to know if his kisses zap you like lightning," Winter taunted.

"Ew!" Spring shrieked. Autumn squealed out loud and Summer put her hands over her mouth to cover her horrified giggles.

"Enough!" Summer finally sputtered. "My turn. Spring, truth or tickle: if you could go anywhere in all the Sparkledoms at this very moment, where would it be?"

Spring answered without even thinking. "My room!"

"Your room?" Winter asked. "In the middle of my Snowflake Slumber Party?"

Winter sounded hurt. Spring hadn't meant to hurt her feelings; she was just playing the game and telling the truth.

Autumn placed a comforting hand on Spring's knee. "Is that true, Spring? Would you rather be in your room?"

Spring didn't know how to answer. She'd already told so many fibs to try and get out of the party, she didn't want to lie anymore. At the same time, she didn't want to upset Winter. Her insides were as twisted as a snail shell and her tongue felt as thick as an elephant's foot. For several moments there were no sounds beyond the wind whipping outside the snow fort and the crackling of the fire.

"I guess that answers the question," Winter said petulantly. "Spring doesn't like my slumber party."

"I didn't say that!" Spring finally exploded. "The game is Truth or Tickle and I was supposed to tell the truth, so I told the truth! I *was* having a lot of fun but you asked where in all the Sparkledoms I would go in that very moment, and the truth was my room! And it's even more true in *this* very moment than that one—*I would like to go to my room!*"

She folded her arms and stared at the fire. She didn't want to meet any of her sisters' stares. Spring did not like Truth or Tickle.

"Fine," said Winter. "Now *I'll* tell the truth. I've done everything I can to make sure this party was super-spectacular for you, but you'd rather be in your room. You're saying my party's not good enough for you?"

"Winter," Summer warned.

"What?" Winter shot back.

"That's not true!" Spring protested. "I had fun before!"

"*Before?*" Winter echoed, offended.

"I have an idea," suggested Autumn. "How about we play another game?"

"Great idea," Summer agreed. "Or we could tell spooky stories, just like Winter planned!"

Suddenly, a strong breeze blew into the fort, extinguishing the fire. Spring yelped loudly. Everything was so dark, she couldn't see her fingers wiggling in front of her face. What if the fort collapsed? What if the Weeds tried to sneak in and steal their scepters?

Spring couldn't breathe. She quickly pulled out her moonstone necklace and chanted softly, "*Little moon, shine bright. Give me comfort in the night.*"

The moonstone transformed into a glowing ball of light that gently illuminated the entire snow fort. All of the Sparkles stared at it in wonder.

"How did you do that?" asked Summer.

"It's from Mother," Spring admitted. "A nightlight to help me at the sleepover."

"Wait," Winter said. "You had to go to *Mother* to get help for the sleepover? Was the idea of a sleepover in my Sparkledom that horrible?"

Spring thought she might be sick. Everything was getting worse and worse, and she didn't know how to make it better. "You don't understand!" she wailed.

"Then help us understand," Autumn said.

"Yeah," Summer said. "If you needed a night-light,

why didn't you just ask us? I'm sure Winter could have given you one."

Tears welled up in her eyes as Spring admitted the truth. "I didn't ask because you would have told me I was a baby, and I wasn't ready for a sleepover. And you'd have been right. I'm *not* ready to talk about which Weed to kiss or to sleep in a snow fort or to tell spooky stories. I'm not ready for a Snowflake Slumber Party, and I don't think I'll ever be ready! I miss Dewdrop. I want to sleep in my own bed and . . . I want to go home!"

Spring ran out of the snow fort. The glowing moonstone lit her way. Outside, giant snowflakes fell from the sky and cooled Spring's hot tears. She could hear her sisters scrambling after her, so she quickly pulled out her scepter and conjured:

"Rainbow, rainbow, speed and zoom,
Take me back to my cozy safe room!"

The colors of the rainbow sparkled through the dark night. They lifted her up and pulled her toward home.

"Spring, don't go!" Autumn's voice rang out behind her. "We'll help you!"

Spring didn't turn around or answer. She let the rainbow take her higher, and by the time Winter's and Summer's voices joined Autumn's, Spring was too far away to even make out the words.

CHAPTER
8

Spring awoke tucked into her own bed. She could feel the Sparkle magic tingling through her body like tiny bubbles. Her powers were always at their strongest the day the season turned to spring. Today she could grow an entire sailboat out of seaweed or a carousel out of carnations.

Normally, she'd bounce out of bed and grab Dewdrop to play with her increased powers, but today she didn't want to.

She only wanted to see her sisters.

She wondered what they were doing. She wondered if they'd gotten a good night's sleep after she left. Most of all, she wondered if they were mad at her for ruining the Snowflake Slumber Party.

Spring tumbled out of bed and looked at her

reflection in the mirror. Her face was puffy from crying and her hair was still in rag curlers. *I definitely look like a little girl who can't even make it through a slumber party*, she thought.

She tugged a few rags out of her hair and sighed loudly. She wished she was as calm as Autumn, as adventurous as Winter, and as brave as Summer.

"Spring! Spring! Spring!"

For a second Spring thought it was one of the animals in her Sparkledom flying by to wish her a Happy First Day of Spring, but the voice sounded far too alarmed. Spring wheeled around and smacked into Serenity, who had soared in through the window. Their collision tangled Serenity's claws in Spring's hair.

"Oh, my goodness, Serenity!" cried Spring. "Are you okay?"

"No!" cried Serenity, flapping her wings furiously to keep her balance. *"Something terrible has happened!"*

"It's not so terrible. You're just a little stuck." Spring soothed the bird as she reached up and held her soft, feathered chest. The turtledove's heart pounded like it was trying to escape her body. "Stay still and I'll help you."

Serenity didn't stay still. She flapped uncontrollably, and Spring winced as the bird tugged and knotted her hair. Her fingers worked as quickly as a spider's legs, trying to ease the tangle, but it only got worse as Serenity kept struggling.

"It's not that, Spring! Mother Nature is under a sleeping spell! And her scepter is missing!"

Spring froze. Fear crawled up her spine like a creeping nightshade. "What did you say?"

Serenity stopped flapping and instead bent over, leaning in front of Spring's head so she could look at the Sparkle upside-down. *"It's true,"* the turtledove sobbed. *"When I went to wake her this morning, I found one of Bluster's chocolates in her hands. It was half-eaten and smelled of valerian root—a powerful sleeping potion! She's fine, but she's not responding to any of my remedies. Bluster must have made it so strong that Mother would stay asleep through sunset and miss the season-changing Ceremony!"*

"And you said her scepter is missing?" Spring asked with dread.

"Yes! So even if we could wake her before sunset, we'd have to do it in time for her to get her scepter back from Bluster!"

"Shivers and shakes!" exclaimed Spring. "If Mother isn't awake with her scepter and able to do the Ceremony by sundown, the season won't turn! The Outworld will stay locked in winter! It will get colder and colder until it freezes solid!"

"I know!" Serenity flapped wildly again, getting more deeply tangled in Spring's hair.

"Ow-ow-ow!" Spring moaned. "Please, let me help you." As Serenity stilled and Spring untangled the dove's feet, she asked, "Serenity, why didn't you go to my older sisters first? Why did you come to me? I can't even make it through a sleepover. How could I possibly know what to do?"

"I came to you, Spring," said Serenity, finally flying free, *"because you understand me. You speak turtledove."*

"Of course," Spring said. "But I can't handle this

alone. I've got to tell my sisters. Will you watch over Mother?"

Serenity promised she would and wished Spring good luck, but Spring was already racing out to the balcony, her scepter drawn:

*"Rainbow race, don't simply glide,
Zoom me to my sisters' side!"*

She leaped into the multicolored beam and crossed her fingers as the rainbow obeyed her spell. It zipped her at lightning speed out of her Sparkle-dom, across to Winter's, and floated her effortlessly right through the roof of Winter's chalet. The sisters were used to the rainbow's power to soar them through solid objects, but Spring's sisters were still startled to see her arrive in Winter's kitchen. The three had been eating breakfast, pouring sparkling syrup on rainbow-colored stacks of pancakes. They were all dressed, and their hair was in curly ringlets.

Winter was the first to notice. "Spring!" she cried.

"Sparkles!" shouted Spring. "I have something to tell—"

Spring couldn't get the words out before Winter vaulted over the breakfast table and pulled Spring into her arms. "I'm so glad you came back!"

That surprised Spring so much, she forgot for a second why she'd raced over there. "You are?" she asked.

"YES!" Winter exclaimed. "I shouldn't have planned such a wild sleepover. It was your very first and I should have been more considerate."

Spring knew Winter hated to apologize, and she was so touched she almost cried.

"It was my fault," Spring said. "I should have been honest about how I felt. I knew I wasn't ready, but I was too afraid to say so."

"But not too afraid to come over with your hair in knots?" Summer teased. "It looks like your head lost a fight with a pricker bush."

Spring's morning came rushing back to her and her eyes grew wide. "Mother!" she gasped. "Bluster Tempest put her under a sleeping spell and stole her scepter!"

"What?" roared Winter.

"How do you know?" asked Autumn.

Spring told her sisters everything. As she shared the tale, a single tear squeezed its way out of her left eye and rolled down her cheek.

"Hey," said Winter, "don't cry. We'll figure this out."

"We sure will," declared Summer. "Bluster Tempest won't get away with this."

"The season will turn today," assured Autumn. "We'll rescue the scepter."

Spring was scared, but her sisters' love and confidence made her feel brave. She wiped her wet eyes. "We *will* rescue the scepter," she agreed. "But how?"

"If I were Bluster"—Autumn shivered at the idea even as she said it—"I'd take the scepter somewhere as hard to find as possible . . ."

"Oh!" Summer remembered. "Mother once told me he has a secret fortress even *she's* never found."

"But if Mother can't find it, how will we?" Spring asked.

"We ask someone who knows," Winter said, smacking her scepter into her palm. "*Four* someones who know. Four *smelly* someones who know. Four smelly, nasty, filthy—"

"In other words, the Weeds," Summer said.

Spring shuddered. The last time they'd tangled with the Weeds, Thunderbolt had broken her scepter. It was the worst moment of her life. Still, if it meant saving Mother and her season . . .

"You're right," Spring said with a voice so strong, her sisters turned and stared. "We'll have to talk to the Weeds, but they could be anywhere. There's only one way to find them quickly, and I'm the one Spar-kle who can make it happen."

CHAPTER
9

"You're doing great," Spring gurgled and hissed to the giant flying snake-creature in his own language. "You're very, very brave."

The four Sparkles were riding on the back of Sammy, a sea monster they'd rescued from the Barrens. Sammy had the body of a serpent, the toothy jaws of a shark, and massive eyes that seemed frighteningly lifeless, but he'd proven he was actually a sweetheart. He lived in Pink Dolphin Lagoon in Spring's Sparkledom now, and if he had his way, he'd never see the Barrens again. Spring had had to work very hard to convince Sammy to fly her and her sisters back there, and to risk running into the terrible boys who'd neglected him so badly. As far as Spring knew, he was the only creature who had lived in that awful place and left. He knew the Barrens well and could help the girls scour it quickly.

Sammy and the girls had been flying over the Barrens for a while now, staring down at the scorched land scarred by constant storms, earthquakes, and tornadoes. They'd passed the castle and moat where the Sparkles had first met Sammy, and were soaring over a new but equally cracked and bleak landscape.

"I see them!" Summer cried.

The other Sparkles followed her gaze toward what looked like a neglected amusement park. A broken-down Ferris wheel, a ramshackle roller coaster, and a creepy carousel with wooden swamp animals all stood scattered like forgotten toys. In the center of the rusted mess, a boiling, stinking mud pool spread like a brown gravy stain, and four boys splashed in the dank, murky water.

"I can't believe they're swimming in that," said Autumn. "It smells like rotten eggs."

"So do the Weeds," Winter noted.

Sammy started to buck through the air, and all four Sparkles held in screams.

"Spring, do something!" Autumn yelped.

Spring understood that Sammy was frightened. The last time he'd flown over the Weeds, they'd tried to hit him with painful bolts of magic. She bent close to his ear and cooed in his screechy language, "Sammy, it's okay. They can't hear you. Remember . . . your wings."

Thanks to the Weeds, Sammy's wings had been in terrible shape when the Sparkles first met him, but now they had grown back so thick and full that they didn't make a sound. The Weeds wouldn't hear him this time.

Comforted, Sammy stopped bucking. He glided the girls in lazy circles around the mud-splashing Weeds. Unnoticed, the sisters watched the Weeds and started planning how they would get the boys to reveal the location of Bluster's secret lair.

Below, pig-nosed Quake sat at the edge of the swamp. He wore a swim cap and an ill-fitting wetsuit, and dipped his feet into the steaming mud while licking a giant stick of candy. Sleet, the angriest-looking Weed, was sprawled belly-down on top of a giant patched inner tube. Twister and Thunderbolt stood on one of Thunderbolt's low storm clouds and prepared to dive into the murk.

Twister went first. He leaped, waved his stick in the air, and shouted, "*Spinnnerrsplattt!*"

His body spun faster than a tornado as he splashed down, making a giant whirlpool that splattered mud everywhere.

"WHOA!" shouted Sleet. He fell off his inner tube and disappeared into the sludge.

Quake was also now completely coated in mud, as was his candy stick. "Twister! Look what you did! I saved that candy in my shoe for a week! I'm gonna pummel you!" He dove into the water and grabbed Twister by his swirl of orange hair.

"Me too!" Sleet yelled. "I was trying to relax!" He threw himself on top of his tussling brothers.

Thunderbolt jumped up and down and cried, "Ooh! I wanna wrestle too!" He belly-flopped off his storm cloud and landed smack on top of everyone. Now all four of the boys were mud wrestling, a tangle of filthy limbs.

"*Boys*," said Summer, rolling her eyes.

"I say we just freeze them," Winter said. Her Sparkle Power turned things to ice, and she pulled out her scepter, ready to use it. "We can tie them up, then thaw them and get them to tell us where to find Bluster's secret fortress."

Yet before she could conjure her powers, several bubbles burbled on the surface of the swamp. Thunderbolt, Twister, and Sleet scattered away from Quake with a chorus of "Ew!" and "Gross!"

"It wasn't that!" Quake complained. "I made an underground quake to get you off me! *That's* what made the bubbles!"

"Yeah, right," Sleet scoffed. "I can smell it, Quake."

"It's a sulfur swamp!" Quake wailed. "That's what you smell!"

The boys kept arguing, but now they were far apart, and Autumn placed a hand on Winter's arm. "You can't get them all at once," she warned. "We don't want to start a big fight. We need to stop them quickly."

"Autumn's right," Summer said. "We each pick a Weed."

"We're gardening?" Spring asked.

"Something like that," said Summer. "Pick which weed you want to pluck. I'll take Sleet."

"I'll grab Thunderbolt," said Winter.

"Twister, please," said Autumn, spinning her scepter.

"Then I'll take Quake." Spring giggled. "That rhymes!"

Winter stood tall on Sammy's back and swung her arms, preparing to leap. "One . . . two . . . three . . ."

"Wait!" Spring stopped her. "We'll have better aim if we swing!" She pulled a few seeds out of the purple pouch dangling around her neck, pointed her scepter at them, and chanted:

"Ropes grow long and let us swing,
We'll grab those weeds and make them sing!"

Violet sparkles enchanted the seeds and four ropy vines grew out of them. She handed each sister her own rope vine and then asked in sea monster language,

"Will you hold the other ends of these for us, Sammy? Tightly, please. Then fly us down so we can get close to the boys."

Spring fashioned two ropes tightly around each of Sammy's wings. Spring knew he'd hold on and keep her and her sisters safe.

"Great idea, Spring," Winter said. "You're amazing."

Spring smiled at the praise, then each sister slid down Sammy's back, holding her end of the rope. They dangled there until each sister was close to her chosen Weed. Winter and Summer let go of their ropes first, and landed right on top of Thunderbolt and Sleet, tackling them in the mud. Autumn touched ground in front of Twister, then blew him out of the slimy pool with a burst of wind.

Quake was the farthest away, and by the time Spring slid off her rope to get to him, he'd crawled out of the ooze and was running through the rusting amusement park. Spring chased him around the carousel, roller coaster, and Ferris wheel, then saw him dodge around some dilapidated dirt bikes. He climbed into a sidecar of one of the bikes and ducked low.

Did he really think he was hiding there? Spring had seen him crawl inside!

She approached slowly, wondering if it might be a trick. With her scepter drawn, she leaned over the top of the sidecar . . . and found Quake cowering on the floor!

"Don't use your scary magic on me!" he wailed. "I've seen what that scepter-thing can do! I don't want any trouble!"

Spring smiled to herself. Quake was frightened because the last time he'd seen Spring's scepter, Thunderbolt had used it. The combination of his powers and hers had created electrified tree roots that were so scary they even terrified Spring.

"I *will* use my scary magic on you," Spring said, "unless you tell me where Bluster Tempest is hiding with Mother Nature's scepter!"

Quake winced. "I can't. He'd be mad if he found out I squealed."

"I won't tell if you don't tell," Spring said.

Quake turned his head to one side and looked up at Spring. A small snail slithered up his cheek. "Honest?" he asked.

"Pinky petal promise," said Spring. She held up the pinky finger on her right hand.

"That's a good promise," decided Quake. "Okay. And promise not to tell my brothers I told?"

"*Double* pinky petal promise," she agreed. She held up both pinky fingers.

The snail had made its way to the tip of Quake's nose. He crossed his eyes to look at it, then whispered, "Bluster hid the scepter in his fortress. It's in the heart of the Parched Desert. It's up in the air, but looks like sand and sky."

Spring sensed that Quake was telling the truth, but she didn't understand. "Is this a riddle? Because normally I love riddles. Like, where do moths go to have fun?"

"Where?" asked Quake.

"To the moth ball," answered Spring. "But right now I don't have time for riddles!"

"I don't get it," said Quake, looking confused.

"Scary magic, remember?" Spring warned, waving her scepter. "Please explain exactly why Bluster's secret fortress is up in the air and looks like sand and sky."

"It's stuck like a piece of spinach between two giant boulders shaped like teeth. It looks like sand and the sky because the whole thing's made of mirrors." Quake eyed Spring's scepter. "I did what you asked. No scary magic now, right?"

Spring felt bad that he was so frightened. After all, her magic wasn't scary and she would never really hurt him. She wanted to do something nice for him, but there wasn't much time. She had to hurry to save Mother's scepter and wake her before sundown.

Then she remembered how upset Quake had been when Twister had muddied his candy stick, and knew she could make him happy in no time at all. She pointed her scepter at the ground and recited:

"Field of candy, suckers, and treats,
sprout up from the earth with a taste
so sweet!"

Violet sparkles tilled the earth and grew into a field of tall green stalks. Each one rose high into the air and blossomed with sucker sticks, chewy taffy, chocolate candy bars, and giant gumballs.

Quake wiped his face in amazement, actually making it dirtier. He also managed to wipe the snail onto his hand. Spring was relieved it had its shell to protect it. "Gee, Spring," he said, drooling. "Thanks!"

As Quake dove into the crop of treats, Spring raced to gather her sisters. She found them back at the swamp. Summer, Winter, and Autumn held Sleet, Thunderbolt, and Twister at scepter-point. The three Sparkles were wind-blown and coated in frost and mud, but the boys were in worse shape. They were encased in ice from the neck down, stopped in mid-run.

"We'll never tell you where Bluster hid Mother's scepter!" Twister yelled.

"Then you'll stay frozen forever!" Winter roared.

"Sparkles!" Spring beckoned to her sisters and they gathered around her. "I know where the fortress is!"

"How'd you find out?" Winter asked.

Spring held up both her pinkies. "Can't say. But I can get us there. Let's go!"

"How?" Autumn asked. "Sammy was so spooked, he already flew back to Pink Dolphin Lagoon!"

Poor Sammy, thought Spring. She couldn't blame him for heading back to her Sparkledom. She wished she could fly back there too. But she and her sisters had a scepter to retrieve.

"I know *exactly* how we'll get there," she said.

CHAPTER
10

Dust kicked up behind three dirt bikes as the Sparkles zoomed along the Parched Desert. Spring led the way on her black cycle with snakeskin decals. Autumn followed on a bicycle with one monster-sized wheel in the front and a mini wheel on the back. Summer's ride had three thick wheels, and Winter bumped

along next to her in a bullet-shaped sidecar. In her mind, Spring thanked Quake. Not only had he told them how to find Bluster's fortress, but he'd led them to the perfect way to get there—the Weeds' dirt bikes!

Spring was also glad she'd rewarded him with the candy patch. It kept him busy, so he hadn't bothered them when they drove away. The other Weeds were still in ice when they left. Winter promised they'd melt free later in the day.

"We've been riding for a long time!" Autumn shouted. "Will we be there soon?"

"I think so!" Spring shouted back.

"We'd better be!" Summer yelled. "There's only a few more hours left for the season-changing Ceremony!"

All four girls scoured the desert plains. A shimmer of heat grazed land as red as a scraped knee, stretching out endlessly in every direction. Boulders stood like sentinels along the way, but none of them looked like teeth, until . . .

"I see them!" Winter hollered. "There!"

Twin boulders rose from the desert floor. They

looked like the fangs of a giant shark buried beneath the sand. According to Quake, the fortress should be between them, but invisible because it was made of mirrors.

"Let's get closer!" Spring suggested.

She and her sisters pumped their pedals and pulled alongside the boulders. Sure enough, their own reflections gleamed back at them.

"Tendrils and tadpoles," Spring cried, "we look a fright!" Spring's hair was still hopelessly tousled and knotted from her tangle with Serenity, and the mud splattered all over her sisters had hardened into a cracked paste.

"Forget that—we found the mirrored fortress!" Winter crowed. "Now we just have to find the door and get in."

"How?" Autumn asked. "The door will be mirrored too. We won't be able to see it."

"We could if we had a tub," Spring said. "The mirror in my bathroom always mists up when I take a bubble bath, and then I can see it really well."

"Spring, that's perfect!" Summer cried.

"A tub?" Spring asked. "It *would* be nice. Then I could wash my hair, and you could get the mud off you, and—"

"Not the tub, the *mist*!" Summer clarified. "If we work together and coat the mirrored fortress in mist, everything on it will stand out—including the door!"

"I love it!" Winter crowed. "How do we make it work?"

"Winter," Summer began, "you create freezing water. I'll heat the air around it to make mist, and Autumn, you blow the droplets so the mist swirls all around the fortress."

"What can I do?" asked Spring.

"Look for the door," said Summer. She pointed her scepter into the air. "C'mon, girls, let's make some mist!"

Winter and Autumn lifted their scepters and they all chanted together:

> "Winter ice and summer heat
> Brew a mist when soon they meet!
> Autumn winds blow through the air
> And reveal Bluster Tempest's hidden lair!"

Following Summer's plan, the three Sparkles used their powers to create a fine mist. As Autumn blew it around and around the space between the boulder "teeth," a pointy structure with towers and columns emerged.

"I see it!" Spring cheered. "Keep misting! I'll find the entrance!"

She furiously zipped her bike around the fortress. Its mist-coated spikes and fang-like overhangs made Spring shiver even in the desert heat. She had held her own with Bluster yesterday, but that was in Mother's Sparkledom, where she felt safe. Did she really want to see him in his own frightening fortress?

Then she turned a corner and all her worry gave

way to excitement. The mist clung to the outline of a door! "Sparkles!" she called. "I found the entrance!"

Within seconds, Spring's sisters were at her side. Together they turned the knob, pushed open the heavy door, and slipped into Bluster's lair. There was a resounding *BOOM* as the door closed behind them.

Inside, the fortress was bone-white, and clean as a skeleton picked over by a pack of hyenas. Staircases that looked like rows of jagged teeth spiraled up and down, leading to wide-mouthed darkened hallways.

"I think I liked it better when it was invisible," Spring quavered.

"There are so many floors," marveled Summer. "So many places to look. We should probably split up."

"Do we have to?" Spring asked.

"Only if we want to get Mother's scepter in time for the Ceremony," Winter said.

Spring looked down at her feet. Of course she wanted to get the scepter in time for the Ceremony. She just didn't want to explore Bluster Tempest's fortress alone. Being in his secret lair made her jittery as a leaf blowing in a fall wind.

"How about this?" Autumn offered. "We'll explore, while you stay and guard the entrance."

"And if you see anything sketchy, call out like a bar-headed goose," said Winter. "Honk! Honk!"

The honk made Spring smile, but she was still nervous. She didn't want to be by herself, but at least she wouldn't have to go deeper into the fortress. She nodded, then her sisters gave her a quick hug before zooming off along three different staircases. Spring hoped they didn't fall into any traps. The Weeds loved booby traps, so it made sense that Bluster would too.

Spring stared at all the staircases. If there was a trap around, maybe she'd see it herself. Then she could honk to her sisters and warn them.

Spring didn't see anything, but the more she concentrated on the staircases, the more she realized that they rose in an ever-widening funnel. The pattern continued when she looked down. Here the stairs narrowed, swirling to a darkened point. In fact, the more Spring studied the fortress, the more it seemed like even the walls spiraled slightly, just like the staircases.

Willows and windstorms! Spring thought to

herself. *Bluster's fortress is shaped like a tornado!* She considered this a moment. *If I were hiding in a tornado, where would I go?*

Suddenly the answer seemed so obvious she said it out loud. "Where would *I* go? The *eye* of the tornado!"

Spring almost honked for her sisters, but she stopped herself. If she was wrong, she didn't want to pull them away from their explorations—not when one of them might be about to find Mother's scepter.

No. She'd check for herself. She'd be careful and stay hidden, and if she *did* see Bluster in the "eye of the tornado," *then* she'd get her sisters.

She tiptoed to the nearest downward staircase and placed her foot on the step.

CRRRREEEEAK!

Spring jumped back. The staircase was no way to stay hidden. She needed to be stealthy, like when she and her sisters slid down from Sammy and surprised the Weeds. She pulled a maple seed pod—a whirlybird—out from the pouch around her neck. She placed it in her open palm, then pointed her scepter at it as she whispered:

> *"Whirlybird seed grow big with might,*
> *Into my hand so I can take flight!"*

Violet sparkles coated the
seed, and it grew into an enormous whirlybird, so large it
stretched up above her like a heli-
copter's rotor.

"Now for a little light to
show the way," said Spring.
She pulled out her moon-
stone necklace from beneath
her nightgown and whis-
pered, *"Little moon, shine bright. Give me comfort in
the night."*

The necklace cast a brilliant glow over the walls
of Bluster's lair. She took a deep breath, then, holding tightly to the whirlybird stalk, she leaped over
the edge of the stairwell. The giant seed pod spun her
gently down to the ground, where she landed on a
round metal disc. The disc had handles—it looked like
some kind of cap in the middle of the floor—and
carved into it was a single eye.

The eye of the tornado! Spring had been right! She again wanted to call her sisters, but the eye didn't mean Bluster or the scepter was here. She needed to keep exploring. She lifted the cap by its handles to reveal a hole, and a golden slide that dove into its depths.

Spring set aside the cap and stretched her moonstone into the hole. She saw that the slide took a sharp turn, then continued beyond the light's glow.

If Spring wanted to know what was down there, she had only one choice. She eased her way onto the slide, then pushed off and plummeted down its slippery slope.

Down and down she went. The spinning ride down the slide was even longer than her whirlybird trip into the eye of the tornado. And even scarier! Lodged into the walls were golden statues of frightening sea creatures poised to attack. Giant squid statues reached out their tentacles, schools of great white sharks bared their razor teeth, and immense anacondas twisted around the slide as if they were about to squeeze the life out of their prey. Spring screamed the whole way down.

THUMP.

Spring landed on her seat. She was afraid to open her eyes, but when she did, she found herself in a greenhouse. It was bright, warm, quiet, and filled with the kind of plants some thought were dangerous, though Spring knew they were simply equipped to defend themselves. Poison ivy drooped from the roof, giant flytraps swelled out of planter boxes, and flowered poison snakeroot blossomed in ghostly white patches. She noticed the greenhouse windows were patterned like a spider web, and she was marveling at their beauty when she realized that right in the center was Bluster Tempest himself, sneering at Spring like a spider who had just caught a wee fly.

CHAPTER
11

Bluster tilted the black rim of his top hat. "Salivations and salutations, Spring!" Over his regular black suit and cape, Bluster wore a white gardener's apron and gloves. He held a tiny pot containing three Venus flytraps. He petted them affectionately, and Spring could hear their pleased purring.

"I must say, my dear," Bluster continued, "you look as fresh as a pile of hay after it's been eaten, consumed, and deposited by a camel."

Bluster gingerly placed the tiny pot of flytraps on a high table next to him, then removed his gloves and pulled an impossibly large black walking stick from one of his apron pockets. He wasn't acting mean. He was polite and even nice, but that frightened Spring all the more. She had no idea what to expect.

"I'm sure you're aware that if I wanted to, I could do away with you immediately," he said. "I suppose you're remarkably terrified."

Spring was, but then she remembered how Bluster had acted when she stood up to him at Mother's. He had been impressed with her then. Maybe she could impress him again, and buy some time while she figured out how to find and rescue Mother's scepter.

"Knock, knock," blurted Spring.

Bluster's smile flickered. "I'm sorry, perhaps you didn't understand. I just threatened you. Are you actually telling a joke?"

"*Knock, knock,*" Spring insisted.

"Fine." Bluster smiled again, his shark teeth even sharper than Spring remembered. "Who's there?"

"Spider."

"Spider who?"

"Spider what everyone says, I like you!"

Spring forced a smile. Saying she liked Bluster was hard, even in a joke, but she thought Bluster would appreciate it.

"Clever," he said. "And true, no doubt. No one can resist me. And I happen to like you too, Spring. I find you both amusing and clever. In fact, right now I'd say you're a particular favorite of mine."

Spring heard the three Venus flytraps cry out, "*She can't be your favorite, Daddy! We are!*"

The flytraps snapped at her jealously. Spring tried not to recoil. "Now it's your turn," she said to Bluster. "You tell a joke. It's a game. You like games, don't you?"

Bluster leaned in close to Spring. His breath smelled like garlic and old pond water. "I. Love. Games. I accept your challenge."

"Challenge?" Spring asked. "I—"

"Knock! Knock!" Bluster rapped his walking stick so loudly on the flytraps' table that the plants' pot bounced up into the air and the flytraps screamed in fright.

"Um . . . who's there?" Spring inched her way toward a table filled with potted hemlock, trying to put it between her and Bluster.

"Spider," said Bluster.

"But I just did that one."

"*Spider!*" Bluster demanded.

"Spider who?"

"You tried to hide her, but I *spied her*!" exclaimed Bluster. "Just like I spied you and your sisters the second you came into my fortress."

"Are my sisters okay?" Spring asked, trying to keep her voice from shaking.

"They're fine, of course. I find it far more enjoyable to keep this between you and me. We *are* friends, after all."

"If I'm your friend," Spring asked, "then why would you stop my season from coming? Without spring, nothing in the Outworld will grow again."

"Not true." Bluster laughed. "The snowfall will grow and grow and grow!"

The plants in Bluster's greenhouse guffawed along with their father.

"But plants won't grow." Spring raised her voice so all the greenery could hear. "Outworld plants just like you will die if there's never any spring."

All the flowers, leaves, and pods quivered. Then they started complaining. Loudly. Bluster's dark eyes stormed over and he shouted out like thunder, "Quiet!"

Not one plant peeped.

Bluster placed his hand dramatically on his heart. "Spring," he said, "it's in my dashing nature to destroy." He aimed his walking stick at a pot of purple flowers. A jet of black smog singed them into ash. The flowers next to the destroyed blooms shrieked horribly. Spring wanted to cover her ears, but instead she stood tall.

"How could you do that to innocent plants under your care?" Spring asked.

"Innocent?" Bluster echoed. "Those flowers were belladonna, a potent poison. Terribly dangerous."

"And what about Mother Nature?" Spring countered. "Is *she* dangerous?"

Bluster smirked and coiled his mustache around his finger. "Not in the same way, no."

"But you betrayed her too," Spring accused. "You left her under a sleeping spell and stole her scepter! And she was your friend!"

"She *is* my friend, Spring," said Bluster Tempest. "A very dear friend."

"I don't believe you," she said. "You deceived her.

And it's not good to deceive a friend. I should know. I ruined Winter's Snowflake Slumber Party because I tried to deceive my sisters and make them think I was ready for a sleepover when I wasn't."

Bluster stared hard at Spring, then spun himself around so fast he became a mini tornado. The Blusterstorm whirled around the room, knocking down and thrashing plants along the way. He stopped inches away from Spring. His hair was tousled and his eyes were wild as he sneered down at the Sparkle and spoke through clenched teeth. "Want to know what you *are* ready for?" he asked.

"What's that?" squeaked Spring.

"Another joke," he said. "But this time we are upping the stakes in this game."

"You're making us steaks?" Spring asked, confused. "I'm not really hungry."

"*Stakes.* As in the stakes, the risk, the gamble, the reward. A scepter for a scepter." He took off his top hat, reached inside, and pulled out Mother Nature's scepter.

"That doesn't belong to you!" shouted Spring. "That's Mother's!"

"Obviously," he drawled. "And if you wager your own scepter, you can win it back for her. Whoever tells the cleverest joke takes *both* scepters. Are you in?"

Bluster set Mother's scepter on a table. Spring gazed at it, then looked at her own. Both scepters' orbs were all but completely clouded in silvery mist. She needed to get them both to the Ceremony right away, or her season would be lost forever. She laid her scepter down next to Mother's. "I am."

"Good," Bluster sneered.

"Wait—how will we know who tells the cleverest joke?" asked Spring.

"My plants will tell us. You are an impartial audience, aren't you, my loves?"

"We love Bluster Tempest!" Spring heard them all sing out.

"Thank you, pets," he said. "Spring, you may go first. And may you have as much luck as a snowman in the desert."

Spring was in trouble, yet she had no choice but to try. At least she knew plants better than Bluster. Maybe that would help?

"Thank you, I think," said Spring, stalling for time as she racked her brain for the perfect joke. "Well, I could tell another knock-knock joke, but I think this time I will tell a story joke."

She knelt next to a planter box filled with tiny white flowers that hung like mini bells on green stems. "I could tell a joke about a world with no spring, but these lovely lilies of the valley only blossom in spring, so I know they wouldn't find that funny at all."

"*No, we wouldn't!*" agreed the flowers.

Bluster tapped his foot impatiently. "You're stalling!" he barked. "If you're telling a story joke, tell it!"

"Pitcher plants and poison ivy!" exclaimed Spring. "You don't have to be louder than an elephant seal's burp to get my attention!"

The lilies of the valley tittered, and the poison ivy hanging from above laughed out loud. Spring started to get an idea.

"I'm hardly that loud," said Bluster.

"Well, you *are* that scary. You're so scary that your own shadow ran away from you."

All the plants in the room gurgled and guffawed.

Spring hadn't tried to tell a joke that time, she just told the truth about Bluster... and the plants thought it was hysterical. *They think it's funny to joke about Bluster,* thought Spring. It was hard for her to tease, but if she had to do it to save her season, she would. Maybe this could be her key to the contest.

"Bluster Tempest, you're so scary, you make onions cry!" exclaimed Spring.

More laughter, especially from the beds of garlic, horseradish, and Brussels sprouts.

"Was that your joke?" asked Bluster testily.

Spring ignored the question. "You're also so mean," she announced to the greenhouse, "that if someone kicked you in the heart, she'd break her toe! You're so icky, the tide wouldn't even bring you in; so frightening, you have to sneak up on your own mirror; so terrifying that farmers use a picture of your face on their scarecrows!"

All the plants were roaring now, rolling back and forth in their pots. One hemlock plant's screeching wail was so loud it cracked the greenhouse glass. Spring couldn't even hear herself over the hysterical din. Bluster smiled through the hilarity at first... then grit his teeth... then small black tornadoes of fury whirled off his body. The sight was terrifying, but Spring acted as though she didn't notice. She waited for the plants' laughter to die down a bit, then put her hands on her hips.

"*That* was my joke," she said. "What's yours?"

Bluster painted on a smile and turned to the crowd of greenery. "Why," he asked, "is the mushroom always invited to parties?" He smiled as if he had the most excellent secret and then answered, "Because he is a *fun guy*! Like me!"

Nothing. Not a chuckle, titter, or snicker. Spring looked around the silent greenhouse, amazed that not one of his poisonous and prickly plants had laughed. Hope stirred inside her.

"*Fun guy*," continued Bluster Tempest. "Like *fungi*. Another word for mushroom." He tapped his walking stick loudly on the mushroom terrarium. "That is your cue to laugh! Laugh, fungi!"

One mushroom offered a pathetic chuckle. Otherwise, silence.

"You are all as humorless as mollusks at a clambake!" Bluster roared.

"So I win!" Spring dashed to the two scepters, but before she could grab them, Bluster pointed his walking stick at her.

"Winds!" he shouted.

A thick, black gust threw Spring across the room, and the poison ivy vines grabbed her in midair. Spring struggled in their grip.

"That's not fair!" Spring shouted. "You said I'd get the scepters if I won!"

"I also told you before . . . *I cheat*."

Spring was furious. She felt her Sparkle Powers rising like a river fed by a giant waterfall. She was *not* going to let Bluster Tempest keep Mother Nature's scepter. Or stop spring from turning. Her own scepter was all the way down on the table, but she was strong enough today that just being in the room with it would be enough. She cried:

> *"Plants and flowers heed my command,*
> *Grow up big and lend me a hand!*
> *Whether with leaf, or your vines,*
> *or poisonous flowers,*
> *Capture Bluster, so he has no powers!"*

A flurry of violet sparkles flew from Spring's scepter and raced around the room, showering each plant and flower with its power. All the creepers, shrubs, and weeds quickly grew larger. As a single group they turned, and while they had no faces, it was easy to see they were glaring at Bluster Tempest.

"Oh, come now," Bluster clucked, "you're not going to obey the magic of a little—"

All at once they pounced. A giant branch of oleander tripped Bluster, then poison ivy vines hoisted him off his feet. They shook him until his walking stick dropped out of his hands.

"Put me down at once!" demanded Bluster.

On his command, the vines plopped him into the mouth of an enormous flytrap. "Not here!" Bluster wailed.

The other poison ivy vines, meanwhile, gently lowered Spring back to the ground and released her. She ran and grabbed her and Mother Nature's scepters, then kicked Bluster's walking stick under a table. Her spell was working and the plants were rebelling! Now to find her sisters and get back to Mother!

"Spring!" Bluster shouted. "You can't win this way! You might have the scepter, but I'm the only one who can wake her up in time for the season to turn!"

Spring stopped in her tracks. It was ⟶
turned back to Bluster. Even though he s
the mouth of the flytrap, keeping its pod op
his feet, and even though his arms were bou
vines, he smiled smugly. Maybe Bluster *had* wo

Spring had run out of clever tricks. All she
left was the truth.

"Mother always told me you were importa
Spring said, her voice trembling. "Just like drought
hailstorms, and sinkholes are important."

"She said that?" asked Bluster Tempest.

"She did. She said we needed you and the Weeds
to keep the world in balance. Just like sometimes a
forest needs a fire to open up the seeds in a pine-
cone, so new trees can be born."

"I do create fabulous forest fires," he mused.

"I didn't want to believe it, but Mother was right,"
said Spring. "I need you. But you need me too, if you
want the plants to release you. So let's work together.
Let's change the season to spring."

Spring wasn't sure if it was her words or the toxic
liquid from the giant flytrap, but Bluster was definitely misty-eyed. "My dear Spring, your words have

loved me like a dish of overripe prunes. We *will* work together. Have the plants release me and I will do as you say. I will wake Mother Nature so you, your sisters, and she can awaken spring."

Spring practically bubbled over with joy, and was about to release Bluster when she remembered his treachery with Mother Nature. If he could turn against his own dearest friend, how could she trust him to do what he said?

At that moment, Winter, Autumn, and Summer came tumbling down the slide and into Bluster's greenhouse, screaming Spring's name. The girls fell into a pile, their legs and arms knotting together like the braid in Dewdrop's mane. As they scrambled to untangle, they all spoke on top of one another.

"Are you okay?"

"We heard shouting!"

"Don't even think of touching her, Bluster!"

The sisters made it to their feet in attack stance, their scepters pointing at Bluster Tempest. Their brows furrowed as they took in the scene: Bluster trapped by his own plants, and Spring standing free. Spring

smiled and held up Mother Nature's scepter. "Ta-da!" she cheerily exclaimed.

"Salivations and salutations, Sparkles!" greeted Bluster. "Although not as adorable as young Spring here, you all look as darling as a pack of donkeys just back from a long uphill pack trip. Now if you don't mind, could you rustle up a rainbow so we can attend to Mother Nature and turn the Outworld's worrisome winter to sunny spring?"

Summer lowered her scepter and leaned on it to keep from falling over.

Winter had only one word: "Honk!"

"Bluebells and blossoms," Autumn gasped, and smiled in amazement at Spring.

Spring wondered if Mother Nature felt this happy when she beat Bluster at cyclone checkers. She knew she wouldn't have to wait long to find out.

CHAPTER
12

Spring proudly stood in the very center of Evergrass Circle with her sisters and Mother Nature. The Sparkle Ceremony was almost complete. Spring lifted her scepter into the air and confidently summoned her namesake season:

"Hear our voices sing, turn winter into spring!"

The other Sparkles joyfully repeated Spring's chant, and their collective Sparkle energy bubbled up and exploded from their headband gems into the orbs on their scepters, then streamed across the field and into Mother Nature's scepter orb.

As Mother stood there, holding their combined energy within herself, Spring thought she looked like a beautiful tree, with her green gown of tiny soft leaves and her brown branch-like arms lifting her scepter up to the sky. Spring's excitement fluttered inside her tummy like a butterfly about to burst from a cocoon.

"Three, two, one . . . ," she whispered.

A brilliant multicolored light shot out of the emerald in Mother Nature's headband and jettisoned into the sky, which exploded with violet and pink fireworks in the shapes of flowers, bees, and leaves. Mother Nature and the Sparkles had done it! Spring had arrived in the Outworld, and nature was balanced once more.

"Bravo, Mother Nature! Bravo, Sparkles!" cheered Bluster Tempest. He stood on the edge of Evergrass Circle. Bits of vine still hung around his ankles and wrists. Spring had known better than to trust his word, so she had the vines in his greenhouse give her cuttings that would answer only to her. With these she kept Bluster tied up until she and her sisters could get him to Mother Nature. Only when Bluster had awakened Mother with his special extra-smelly smelling salts did Spring release him.

Spring was sure Mother would be furious with

Bluster when she learned what had happened, but she had only smiled. "Treachery is what I expect from you, Bluster," she'd said. "I'd be disappointed by anything else. Luckily, I can count on my strong, brilliant, caring Sparkles. You especially came through for us today, Spring. I'm very proud of you."

Spring had glowed under Mother's praise, but by then it was nearly sundown. Mother only had just enough time to magically clean and dress the Sparkles before the Ceremony, which she insisted Bluster and his Weeds watch.

The Weeds were there now, slumped next to Bluster. They wore stained suits and poked and kicked at one another.

"Boys," Bluster urged, "aren't you going to tell Mother and the Sparkles what a lovely job they did?"

"Uh . . . good job," mumbled Thunderbolt.

"Cool ceremony," muttered Twister.

"Yeah, what he said," groused Sleet.

"I liked the fireworks!" enthused Quake. He was licking a giant sticky jawbreaker, and Spring was sure it was from his personal field of candy.

"I'm so glad you boys enjoyed it," said Mother. "Especially since it so nearly didn't happen."

Bluster bowed his head under Mother's stern glare. "What can I say? I am who I am. I trust this mishap won't get in the way of our next Game Night?"

"Of course it won't," Mother said. "Defeating you at cyclone checkers will be the perfect way to exact my revenge."

"Defeating me?" Bluster laughed. "Oh, no, no, no. I assure you, that won't happen."

As he and Mother continued talking and the Weeds started to wrestle, Spring gathered her sisters. She had something on her mind.

"Winter, Autumn, Summer," she said, "with everything that happened today, I never really got to say how sorry I am that I ruined the Snowflake Slumber Party. I know I should have been honest and told you I wasn't ready for a sleepover, but I didn't want you to think less of me. I know I'm the littlest, but I want to be brave like the three of you."

"Brave like the three of us?" asked Autumn. "Spring, you're the bravest!"

"You faced Bluster Tempest all by yourself . . . and won!" agreed Summer.

"Spring . . . you saved spring!" Winter cried.

All three of Spring's sisters wrapped her in a huge hug. Spring could almost feel herself growing taller as she soaked up their love and pride.

Suddenly Winter gasped. "The baby animals! Is it too late to name all of them?"

"Not at all!" said Spring. "They'll be waiting in Goldenseal Grove!"

"I want to name the first baby bunny India Rose!" said Autumn.

"I love that!" Summer cooed. "I want to name a baby duckling!"

Summer, Winter, and Autumn all pulled out their scepters. Spring did not. She was deep in thought.

"Spring?" Summer asked. "Aren't you coming?"

"You know what?" Spring said. "I think now I *am* ready for a sleepover."

"Snowflake Slumber Party Part Two!" Winter cheered. "Let's do it tonight! You want to?"

"Bluebells and blossoms, yes!" cried Spring.

The sisters smiled together, then raised their scepters in the air to summon the rainbow.

"First the animal-naming ceremony and then my very first sleepover," said Spring. "An adventure we'll never forget!"

Elise Allen is the author of the young adult novel *Populazzi* and the chapter book *Anna's Icy Adventure*, based on Disney's *Frozen*. She cowrote the *New York Times* bestselling Elixir trilogy with Hilary Duff, and the Autumn Falls series with Bella Thorne. A longtime collaborator with the Jim Henson Company, she's written for *Sid the Science Kid* and *Dinosaur Train*.
www.eliseallen.com

Halle Stanford, an eight-time Emmy-nominated children's television producer, is in charge of creating children's entertainment at the Jim Henson Company. She currently serves as the executive producer on the award-winning series *Sid the Science Kid*, *Dinosaur Train*, *Pajanimals*, and *Doozers*.

Paige Pooler is an artist who loves to draw pictures for girls. You can find Paige's artwork in *American Girl* magazine and the Liberty Porter, Trading Faces, and My Sister the Vampire middle grade series.
www.paigepooler.com

The Jim Henson Company has remained an established leader in family entertainment for over fifty years and is the creator of such Emmy-nominated hits as *Sid the Science Kid*, *Dinosaur Train*, *Pajanimals*, and *Fraggle Rock*. The company is currently developing the Enchanted Sisters series as an animated TV property.
www.henson.com